Littl

By Malaika De Nur

A Collection of Poems Empowering Women & Girls

This book is dedicated to my mother, my daughters, sisters (biological and not), nieces; and to all the other dynamic women, I know, that chose and continue to choose to triumph over tragedy.

M. D.N.

Contents

Contents

Contents

Introduction

Inside of every woman there is a little girl. A girl that was once innocent and delicate. She grows up, yet she never ceases to exist. She always resides on the inside. She represents many emotions including overflowing love, fear, happiness, anger and sadness. That little girl is a safe space. For it was once okay for her to make mistakes, to consider everyone good and not consider herself prey.

The little girl experiences love, and she experiences heartbreak. She must fight for everything. She learns that she can overcome all the things she once feared. She can win all the battles she lost in the past. She is beautiful, wise, and invincible. For her true power remains within. If she ever forgets her strength, all she must do is close her eyes and remember that little girl.

For that little girl is the key to her resilience over restlessness. She can initiate intelligence over ignorance. She can persevere over punishment. She can select strength over stress. *That little girl* knows how to triumph over tragedy.

This book is about empowering girls and women to believe in themselves. I want all girls and women to know that there is no struggle too vast to overcome. We should be empowered to speak up about our challenges, share with one another, forgive ourselves for past mistakes, and use our adversity as a stepping stone for future success.

Chapter One: Precious Jewels

Being part of the natural world reminds me that innocence isn't ever lost completely; we just need to maintain our goodness to regain it.

-Jewel (Jewel Kilcher, Singer)

Little Jewels

There is much to learn
From the little girls inside us.
All the lessons we forgot,
They will remind us.

Like don't take no shorts
Go for the whole bag.
And if you fall too short
You can always make a comeback.

That little inner voice
Holds many secrets
She knows when to reveal
Or when she should keep it.

When life hits you hard
Channel the impact.
When they say you can't,
Give them some push back.

Your innocence isn't all lost
It's now your conscience.
When you know something is right
On those things, you don't bend.

Reach for the stars,
Don't settle for the sky
If you can't get to Mars,
You can go somewhere close by.

They say you're from Venus
But we are all humans.
So, when you make mistakes
Forgive yourself and improve then.

Whenever you get lost,
Know she's right behind you.
You will never stray too far
from the little jewel inside you.

A Girl's Best Friend

You saw her in a reflection
And just new she was the one,
That would always be present
Through all the trials and through the fun.

Someone she could count on
So rare and unique.
To overlook her is a downfall
For on your mountain, she's the peak.

She is always around you.
Keeps you on her mind.
Has your back and your front
You'll never be left behind.

When you think you can't do it
She will assure you that you can.
The voice of your reason
Not just in making demands.

She knows your true purpose
possesses clarity.
To her you are worth it,
It's not just charity.

For she is your best Ally

Your true ride or die
Whenever you feel lonely,
She is there by your side.

If you *have her*
You won't need anyone else.
You can see in any mirror,
You have a friend inside yourself.

Diamonds

When they ask of her strength,
Some say delicate and weak
Which is evidence they don't know
Of that which they speak.

See my girls are brick houses
So sturdy and firm.
If you underestimate them,
Their strength you will learn.

Their beauty is hypnotic
Some say they cast spells.
You will think of them psychotic
When you see them raise hell.

They are like diamonds,
So precious and rare.
Yet you treat them like garbage
Leave them in despair.

They will give you such wealth
If you know their true value.
Still, many disrespect them
Or just don't know how to

See them as humans
Not prizes to be possessed
Diamonds form in nature
They must be freed from their oppressors.

They want to buy and sell them
But they can't prevail over them.
For there is strength in their flaws
Their abrasions will compel them.

Truthfully, their roughness
Makes them exceptional
With brilliance beyond measure
They're quite unconventional.

Sent

Dedicated to my Leena

Like an angel from the heavens
I know why you were sent.
And the timing was so perfect.
That it was clear that you were meant.

To be my joy after the pain
My light inside the dark.
To be the apple of my eye,
My child, you are my heart.

Of all the gifts I have been given
You found a special place.
Upon loves thread, that I share evenly
You tug that string all day.

Tried to take over my heart,
As I say, "you have to share."
You say "sharing is caring"
Then you let the others come near.

You captivate my spirit!
Prove my work is incomplete.
To ensure your brightest future,
I'd endure a mountain peak.

When you rise above my height
And the funds have all been spent
I will say a silent prayer
For this one that Heaven sent.

To Be

For the young girls so rough,
For those who are fancy and free.
There's something you should know
Inside you, there is a key.

You wear your dark colors
You shave your hair off too
But under it all
There's a little girl inside you.

You used to dream big
What happened to that?
A doctor, a ball player
An architect, in fact.

When they say you can't
You must beg to differ.
For your dreams are what
make you, so please reconsider.

When they dare you to go
You must call their bluff.
If they're asking for more
Just say, "I'm enough."

The world can't contain you
So set yourself free.
You shall be whatever it is
You want to be!

Chapter 2: Love Yourself

'Life is really not easy, we all have our
personal battles, but it is important that
you really treasure yourself, love yourself
and have a sense of self-worth.'

– Heart Evangelista (Actress & Philanthropist)

Flawless

Just look at her beauty
Something out of a movie
Lights, camera and action
She passes laws of attraction.

It's not only external
It lies deep within her.
Pristine and so perfect
Not many contend with her.

Though she's not an actor
She remains a factor.
The topic of discussion
Makes hearts beat like percussion.

Her glamor exudes her
But don't dear exclude her
For she is much needed
She gives special treatment.

She knows that she's awesome
Humble when she's flossing
She shares her gifts often
Her eyes, you'll get lost in.

No rules can contain her
You'd consider her lawless.
She governs herself
This woman is flawless.

Renaissance Woman

Rose through ashes like a phoenix
Although most would not believe it.
They can't see the wounds that I healed,
They don't know how I achieved it.

Something brought me back to life
When my heart stopped beating.
Heard the words of ancestors
Went to war with all my demons.

This rebirth is something special
Living here on this borrowed time
One moment you are here
Next, you're running out of time.

Since I knew that time was precious,
I just cut right to the chase.
I chose to live my dreams
Before I leave this place.

I can swim across the oceans,
See no obstacles in my way
What appears to be a threat
Retreats when I walk their way.

They must recognize my blessings
They must see my many gifts.
These here gifts would be of nothing
Without ones to share them with.

So, I'm sharing them with you
In your view, I take a chance.
For I am a powerful woman
And this is my renaissance.

Flawed in My Purpose

No, I am not perfect
I'm so full of flaws.
I follow my heart
more than I follow laws.

I'm scarred by my baggage
I'm broken and bruised.
I am not defeated
So don't be confused.

I laugh at my weakness
And celebrate my strength.
For the ones that I love
I will go to great lengths.

Move Heaven or hell
Move mountains on earth.
Determined to be a blessing
Refuse to be a curse.

A distant ray of sunshine
Will burn you up close
So please keep your distance
Unless you want both.

Take my good and my bad
Take my joy and my pain.
I promise if you take it,
It will not be in vain.

Cause no one is free from
the stains of this life.
You may conceal it with makeup
But the truth is inside.

The truth is my greatness
Will cover my flaws.
My battle for justice
will conquer those laws.

The love that I share
will cover my quarrels.
The wrongs I have done
Will hide behind my morals.

For I have been chosen
for something so great.
To change this here world
With love and not hate.

As I carry out my purpose
Be sure of what you see
My gifts and imperfections,
Are what makes me as me.

Know Your Spirit

I'm not impressed by makeup,
Masks, or other facades
I want to know who is truly you?
Without a poke or prod.

So, show yourself, your real true self
The self beneath your skin
Bring yourself back down to earth
Remove the clothes you're in.

I want to see that heart of gold,
Or what truly makes you tick.
I want to know the real you,
Not the one, you often present.

So, tell me, is there a dark side
Are you flawed like all else in the world?
Show what makes you, who you are
and the truth will be unfurled.

Do you give to charity?
Do you help others in need?
Do you pray for your mistakes?
How often do you do good deeds?

Your heart and soul are who you are.
Not your body although you wear it.
I want what's underneath it all
I want to know your spirit.

No Likes Necessary.

They don't like my smile
They don't like my style
They don't like my happiness
Or anything worthwhile.

Lucky for me, I don't need likes.
I don't need their follows
I know hearing this
is a tough pill to swallow.

I don't need your friendship,
I don't need a Tweet
I don't need fake smiles
Pretending you're sweet.

I don't need no wolves
that are covered in fleece.
I don't need to be validated
Just leave me in peace.

I don't need subscribers
I don't need to be watched.
I'll take me some love,
But be careful with this heart.

It's covered in gold
but it could turn to Steel
In the Media fold,
It's much harder to heal.

Let's go behind scenes
Who needs the limelight?
Let's get to know each other
When the world's out of sight.

Let's add privacy settings
Let's filter our search
Let's believe in ourselves
Even when it hurts.

And now that we're alone
Only one thing left to do
Just look inside the mirror
And say I love you.

My Beauty

Most people wouldn't call me pretty,
at least not conventionally.
I have acne on my face
and stripes on my belly.

I have thin lashes
and very full lips
Of a short stature
with childbearing hips.

Most people wouldn't call me
pretty, at least not conventionally.
I have a dimple on one cheek
and a scar on my knee.

My waist is not too big,
but my thighs jiggle when I walk
Oh, did I forget to mention
that I spit when I talk?

But my mind is open
and my heart is big,
From it genuine love
I am determined to give.

I love God, I love life,
I love friends and family,
I love respect, I love freedom,
I love you and I love me.

Most people wouldn't call me pretty,
not in Winter, Summer, Spring, or Fall.
But if you can't see my beauty,
Then honey, don't call me at all.

Chapter 3: Gifts of a Mother

"Having kids — the responsibility of rearing good, kind, ethical, responsible human beings — is the biggest job anyone can embark on."

-Maria Shriver (Journalist)

A Mother's Burden

Carried the world on your shoulders
Armed like a soldier.
You make it look easy
Even when you grow older.

Who knows of your burdens or
Of your sacrifices.
Only God can bear witness
Most cannot conceptualize it.

For you carried children
That left you with scars.
Yet you kept on living
And you went oh so far.

Such an inspiration to those,
blessed just to know you.
You took no vacation
From shaping and molding.

You taught by example
Gave out a blueprint.
We are still falling short
We'll never know how you do it.

I guess you were chosen
To have this hear journey
Your beauty is frozen
Your love still consoles many.

Queen of the heavens
You reign in your greatness
Demons are jealous,
That you never go faithless.

For you are champion
A hero in your right.
The Angels in heaven,
Would admire your light.

Such big shoes to fill
But heaven is at your feet
So, grow then we shall
to be amongst those that don't grieve.

Ever so graceful
Yet you are a movement.
You can teach a nation.
So glad we're your students.

All We Got
Dedicated to my sweetest little Leena.

Sometimes what we get
is what we got
So, when we got you,
We know we got a lot.

We did not plan you,
But we still chose You.
When everything is fading
Feels good just to hold you.

Searching for old things,
Lost in the source
Your presence is golden
As life takes its course.

If we can't get the love back
Thank God, we have *you*.
To smile and rejoice for
Your purpose is so true.

When nothing else matters
You stay a concern
Throughout all the chatter
Your faith we must learn.

For you believe in us
Your eyes say it all.
With you holding our heart strings
There is no way to fall.

Another Mom
Dedicated to my second mom, Tahira

They say you only get one
But I beg to differ.
No matter where you are
You're always better with her.

For she is your love,
She is your peace.
A mom like no other
Her love is your lease.

A new lease on this life
and in the hereafter.
A pathway to heaven
Your happily ever after

It lies at her feet,
It lies in her example,
She guided so many,
Her care was so ample.

Enough for an entire village
But tailored to those she loved
We shared her with everyone
But she belongs to the one above.

I love you my mom
You welcomed me in your heart.
You showed me such grace
And love right from the start.

I'll always remember the love you gave me
So blessed to have another mom.
Hope these blessings
might save me.

Me Becoming You

How did the roles get so twisted?
When did we make the shift?
The reversal can't be lifted
Is it a curse or is it a gift?

For you were the one who raised me
Took care of all my needs.
Now I have become the caregiver
It is you that now needs me.

If I could turn back the time,
I would have thanked you for your care.
For you were at my service
And at your side, I had no fear.

How is it you can grow up
And then become a child again?
You were once so independent
Now on me you must depend.

When I think of you, so youthful
I start to see myself.
See your vibrance, see your beauty
See you, in so much great health!

It's as if I am you
and now you have become me.
One that needs someone to depend on
I'm independent and I am free.

Yet compelled here as my duty
I must return this gift to you.
While I now care for my own offspring,
I must care for *my caregiver* too.

Mother is Love
Dedicated to my mom, Kareemah

Words cannot explain
the love and joy
this woman brings.

So traditional, yet unconventional
Showed me the potential
Of what the world could be
Beautiful and kind, just like she

Queen of my world
Giver of good deeds
You soften my heart
And you make me believe.

That greatness exists
It lives in our thoughts.
Oh, mother your gifts
Are the battles you fought.

So that I would not have to,
I walk in your shadow.
My guardian angel
For you, I'll face danger.

The womb that so bore me
A couple others before me
But still, you adore me,
Your 3rd to come offspring.

My gentle good nature
It comes from your nurture.
I'll never forsake you,
For you give me purpose.

You give me energy
You give me strength
For Believing in me,
You have gone to great lengths.

For I only know one
that is greater than you,
I pray to him daily
That he looks over you.

Keep you in his favor
And give you your crown
Here and hereafter
When nothing else is around.

You deserve a world beautiful
You deserve all the love.
You deserve such high honor
It must come from above.

A divine recognition
of all your great works.
You swallowed your losses
You smile when it hurts.

You give me such courage
I can face anything
Gave birth to resilience
Overcame so many things.

No challenge too great
No storm was too grand
To weather with gracefulness
On your wings, I stand.

A hero to many
A champion of what's right
My mother, *you see*
You reflect his true light.
Nothing this world can give you

Will value your worth
But enjoy this here offer while you leave
your mark upon this earth.

Always know you are valued
Know you are loved
I love you, my mother
My mother is love.

Chapter 4: Adversity

"When adversity strikes, that's when you have to be most calm. Take a step back, stay strong, stay grounded and press on."

– LL Cool J (Actor/Musician)

Broken Person

I keep wanting to be strong
When I'm feeling very weak.
Been out here hanging with a wolf.
When I'm just a sheep.

Trying to forget about the pain but
I guess trying is not enough.
Because this pain lives in my body
And it encases me like cuffs.

Want to break free of this bondage
That has rendered me inept.
The trauma still lives inside me
In the secret that I kept.

I cannot speak of this disaster,
Though days I wear it on my face
Chasing happily ever after
When my heart is left so scathed.

I've been beaten, bruised and battered
By this, life of mine.
My emotions are so scattered
Can't even walk in a straight line.

Not good enough to meet the standards
Of those I claim to love.
Outcasted out here like a bandit
I pray to the lord above.

Please relieve me of this baggage
I carry such a heavy load
And the weight you could not fathom
Has me ready to explode.

I've been ticking like a time bomb
Just Waiting for the bell
When it rings, I hope my times up
Please relieve me from this hell.

No one will ever understand me
Normal just doesn't apply
Pretend to be like all the others
Why do I even try?

Like an egg upon a tower
My balance is out of whack.
This here wall cannot sustain me
And no one's there to have my back.

I have just fallen into pieces,
Do you even recognize me?
Are you good at solving puzzles?
If so, then you may find me.

You may notice all the scars.
Will you kiss upon my wounds?
Like a mother to her baby
The boo boos will all fade soon.

I guess nothing ever lasts
And true love does not exist.
There is no knight in shining armor.
And there is no magic kiss.

All the noise inside my head
And my feelings that are mixed,
We'll just reside amongst these pieces,
Praying one day we get fixed.

The Great Fall Poem

Who tugged upon my wing
And causeth me to slip.
It must have been the evil one
With his electrifying grip.

He shocks your system gracefully
Wears upon your soul.
Once your guard has lowered well,
He'll swallow your life whole.

He preys upon the innocent
And feast upon the weak.
And if you're caught within his grasp.
It is for him; you now shall speak.

At first, he whispered to you at night
He told you glamorous lies.
Despite your heart being skeptical.
You thought to give them a try.

You did not see his advancement
And this was your greatest mistake.
For those without a watchful eye
He'll surely claim his stake.

He'll never let up on the noose
He placed it upon your neck.
He'll ride you like a vehicle
Until you meet your death.

Had you given, no response to him
And followed your true calling.
You would have been successful
Not of those whom, from grace have fallen.

Deep did you descend yourself
Beyond the depths that you fathomed.
Surely, we would have brought a rope
Or had someone to catch them.

So, keep your eyes on him and
Call upon your savior
Invoke the one who showed you grace,
mercy, and such high favor.

Seek refuge from the evil one.
Do not answer his calls.
His only true intent for you.
Is to watch you as you fall.

You'll Never Know Poem

Dedicated to Alison A. Skeete, Johnnie Williams &
Johanna Nunez

You'll never know how much
you helped me
Cause you were just being you
Like angel in disguise
You did what you came to do.

God-fearing in nature
I could see your holy light.
I could see your loving heart
Your empathy towards my plight.

You gave me my salvation
And you did not even know
The way you lifted me in perspective
Now I can surely grow.

Grow from this situation
Become stronger, become brave
Rise from ashes as a Phoenix
Arise from the trauma unscathed.

Three angels bearing gifts
Like a wise and holy tale.
There was courage, there was strength
There was companionship in your grail.

Bootstraps Poem

They say get up on your feet
Stand up straight and tall.
Pull yourself up by the bootstraps
Break down that heavy wall.

They think that it is easy
To just to put the past behind.
But I'll listen to your reasoning
When your straps weigh a ton like mine.

Heavy is the burden,
Women carry upon their breasts.
Plagued with generations of disadvantage
'Til their souls are laid to rest.

This is not a movie
Life is not a fairy tale.
These boots were made for stomping
Until 'tween their legs, you see their tails.

Only God will be the victor,
In a story such as this.
He can make it so a small army
Deem a great one nonexistent.

Now that small army of women
Will not conquer all of man.
Only ones not found downtrodden
Will be left, we see, to stand.

So, my boots are quite impressive
They have weathered many storms.
But don't tell me to pull the straps up,
until you've walked inside their form.

Fade Into Black

I want to climb out of this hole.
I wanted to reach many goals
Seems like I can't climb no more
Or don't know what I'm climbing for.

Life just hit me so hard
Left me wearing many scars.
Sunk down deep in an abyss
Not quite sure how to get out of it.

I thought there were cushions below
Yet I felt all the blows.
With no Teflon on my chest
Look at me, a bloody mess.

Quite a tizzy of a sought
I was down low and still I fought
Skin grew tough and thick
Yet I'm still in the thick of it.

My favorite color is all I see
Reflecting darkness inside of me
My own mind it frightens me
Watch out for the other side of me!

Now I love me some color black.
But I don't think I'm coming back.
Left that girl I used to be.
Yet she still has her eye on me.

I don't know who you see
Somehow, I'm still surprising me
There is no disguising thee.
I let myself go, so I am free.

So lost in this lonely world
I pray for a lonely girl.
Yet I can't pick up all the slack
I just keep on going back to black.

Chapter 5: Sisterhood

Both within the family and without, our sisters hold up our mirrors: our images of who we are and of who we can dare to become.

-Elizabeth Fishel (Author, Journalist)

Music to Our Ears

Me and my girls here,
We could start a band.
Holding hearts beating
In the palm of our hands.

Rhythmic like drums
Siren calls when we hum.
Moving bodies all around
We make things happen in this town.

Breathed air into you
When you were unseen.
We give people life
like a top magazine.

They will never say thank you,
Good thing we're secure.
We just do what we do
And we keep getting more!

Buy real estate from heads of haters,
We stay inside their minds.
But we're humble by nature,
So, we won't be unkind.

We will always see you
Though you're invisible to most.
They all want to be *us*
On that there, now let's toast.

Cheers to my sisters
That put in that work!
We make it look so good
They believe we don't hurt.

We bleed just like you do
But there is spice in our veins.
Our skin is much thicker
But we still do feel pain.

We laugh at our struggles
We challenge our fears.
And when others say we can't
It's just *music* to our ears.

My Sisters
Dedicated to my sisters

Like life is a runway,
Their strut is so fierce.
Leaving their marks on
Whosoever comes near.

A branding of some sort
A bid to the team
You, they will initiate
And you'll be held in high esteem.

My sisters have knowledge
They learn and they teach,
Concepts greater than scholars
And they practice what they preach.

My sisters protect me.
They always have my back.
If an enemy approaches,
Best believe they will attack.

My sisters are determined
They check goals off one-by-one.
When one door closes
They take windows or build tunnels.

My sisters aren't selfish
Always looking out for the rest.
They give and help others
As a fact, they are selfless.

If one sister falls,
they reach out to pick her up.
They reflect on their blessings
And it's this that fills their cups.

My sisters have accolades
Grander than your wildest dreams.
My sisters cannot fail,
For they are on a winning team!

Wild, Wild, West

Now these here streets
are very mean
We must be strong to survive
We must stay clean.

I've seen them eat folks alive
Like lionesses who fled their pride.
When you think you cracked the code
These blocks will quickly turn the tide.

We need not walk these streets alone
For we have sisters in our home.
When outsiders try to reign
Our sisters surely claim the throne.

We're always armed, go about strapped
In case some cowboys, forget how to act.
My girls, I know they got my back
We're there for each other, that's a fact.

An orange hue could take the sky.
A tumbleweed could go rolling by.
We do not flinch, just quick to draw
We'll leave opponents on the floor.

Only calculated risks, no play of roulette
To approach this team, not a safer bet.
For we live in the wild, wild west.
We learned to fight and eliminate threats.

Unbreakable Bond

Now what could tear at threads so tight?
Some, they try with all their might.
I guess I understand their plot
They wish to stop what can't be stopped.

They look at us and see we're so close.
How could anyone forge such a pact?
My sisters and I, we are a pack.
Like wolves when threatened, we attack.

We wish no harm on anyone.
We spread our love, joy and peace.
Why don't some like such harmony?
They wish to break this treaty.

They cannot break what God has formed.
Many have tried and you've been warned.
These ties right here are formed in gold.
For this sisterhood will never fold.

Why make efforts to destroy
That for which, you are fond.
Just admit and concede
You face an unbreakable bond.

Chapter 6: Triumph Over Tragedy

"The future rewards those who press on. I don't have time to feel sorry for myself. I don't have time to complain. I'm going to press on."

—Barack Obama (Former President/Author)

My Life

I don't know where to start
Or how I should begin
But I also know that giving up
is not a way to win.

So, I'm standing up for justice
I'm doing what is right.
No matter where the chips may fall
I'm taking back my life.

I will not live in silence.
I will not live in fear.
Though I won't resort to violence.
You should watch your back my dear.

Cause Karma's a canine
of the female type.
You may think us females weak
I'm taking back my life.

You will no longer hurt me
You will now feel my pain
You won't get away abusing'
For a measly gain.

To Tell the truth you disgust me
Trying to take what's not yours
But now giving women justice
Is what I'm living for.

No, I can't save them all
Yes, I know there's a price
But I'm geared up for this battle
I'm taking back my life!

Secrets

My friends trust me because they know
I take secrets to my grave.
When the strongest would have folded.
I would have never ever caved.

Know where bodies have been buried,
But it has not escaped my lips.
They try to render you as loose,
But they will not sink this ship.

some tales should not be buried
They must somehow be revealed.
Even if you know when you expose them
How uncomfortable it will feel.

So, get your shovel and listen carefully
Dig this dirt, I say.
Don't let the pain remain buried
Don't let that monster get away.

It's okay to be embarrassed
But don't wear that on your sleeve.
When you work towards your closure,
You will finally start to breathe.

Don't suffocate in your secrecy.

You will need to rally troops.
You will need them in your corner,
So, your life, you can recoup.

So, turn your hideout to a gallery
Showcase all your scars.
Seek help and guidance from around you
This will get you over the bar.

What if all those hidden demons
Come for the women that you love.
You will wish you said that secret
With all of your might to God above.

So here in lies a message,
from loyal bone collectors like me.
There is a time to reveal a secret
And the truth shall set you free.

Darkest Hour

If with a struggle comes some ease
I have something to look forward to.
Cause here inside this moment,
I feel defeated, black and blue.

These aren't colors of the spectrum
With a cauldron of riches at the end
This is not an urban legend.
This me, her, her, and him.

Not the first one to embark upon
This obscure kind of space.
Where you're faced with your emotions
In a depressive kind of state.

Every cloud has silver linings
But some clouds can cause a storm.
It can strip away your power.
You may not feel very strong.

Please don't lose your courage
Find your strength and find your voice
You can talk about what happened.
Because there is no other choice.

Before the ref declares a winner
You stop the clock and raise your hand.
It is in your darkest hour.
That you will rise and take your stand.

Where will you find the courage
Somewhere deep inside your soul?
You will take back your power.
There is light, a pot of gold.

Chapter 7: Victorious

"We are what we repeatedly do. Excellence, then, is not an act, but a habit."

—Aristotle

Head High

Walked right into my destiny
Ordained like you were meant for me
Feels now like I just don't exist
Head high like you told me this.

Snatched away precious Jewels
Stolen like the heart you used.
I fell so in love with you
Head high like I meant to do this.

Master of my universe
Blessings disguised in a curse
You tasted my love for you
Head high like you wanted too

I'm not in control of this
Wheel snatched like a carjacking
I will not be a victim though
Head high like I really know

Just how I slipped into this
Marathon like I'm meant for this
I tasted your potential then
Head high like you knew you'd win.

Resilience I'll come back from it
I let this thing be happening
I drifted into a fantasy,
Head high like l romantically
gave you a piece of me.

Still walking with dignity
Owning my own decisions
Reclaiming my future though
Head high like we knew I'd go!

My Own Hero

I'm not waiting on a Clark Kent
To go change inside his booth.
Not looking for no Parker,
John Wayne, Robin or even Bruce.

They say a hero is just a sandwich
Some meat, some cheese and bread.
But my hero is cut from different cloths
She's wearing the finest threads.

You won't find on my knees
'Less I'm praying to my lord.
Don't bring checkers to a chess game,
For all my queens are on this board.

We don't need knights in Armor.
Or Bond in his fast cars.
For this streetcar you desire,
Will leave most men seeing stars.

So don't play me as no damsel
Please do know, this is no game.
My Hero is wearing high heels,
And she's bearing my own name.

Her Story

Who will tell your story?
Will it be you?
All the fame and the glory
What has it come down to?

Did you do all the things
you set out to do?
Did you face all your fears?
Did you live in your truth?

They say history is told
By the ones who are victors.
Did you achieve your goals?
Were you constricted?

You let no one hold you back
You stepped out of your shell.
On the way straight to heaven
You walked through some hell.

Yet you rose from the ashes
You pursue your dreams.
When it came to a challenge,
You changed it to a meme.

You laughed at it later
Forgave yourself too
You moved with grace
As your soul compelled you.

You wear all the bruises
Memorized all the tales.
You used your own wit
When everything else failed.

Who will tell her story?
In all its true glory
Her beauty, her patience,
Well into her forties.

Well, you know the answer
It lies within you.
So, give them the facts
Speak to them in truth.

For her true story
is glorious.
You will tell your own,
As you are victorious.

Standing By Rights

When our vote could not be cast
When our place was behind closed doors.
There were visionaries and women
that fought for so much more.

They did not want you wearing pants
They told you, "Stay inside your place."
If your skin was made of color,
The double whammy was your race.

Yet you put on your trousers on
You stepped out of your bloomers.
You went to work in the fields.
Refused to be merely a consumer.

You took breadcrumbs for your pay
While to men, the dollars were many.
You continued to pray,
Until your few grew into plenty.

You have traveled centuries,
Expecting life to be much different.
Susan B would be shifting in her grave
To see the life, we now are living.

The pay is more, but not even

In fact, you may not get the job.
They think when work gets hard
All the women will do is sob.

I leave tears drenched on my pillow,
Before I walk outside my door.
You will not see me cry
As I fight to change these laws.

Still rolling back our rights.
You want to take away our choice.
Go get your rifles, line them up
You will not silence our voices.

How can you give me protection?
You're the one that I should fear.
Only reason I don't fear you is,
because God got me my dear.

If it's war you want, get ready
We will fight the worthy fight!
We will not stand by idly
And let you take away our rights.